MAR 22

BUBBLECAT vs. DRAGONBEAR

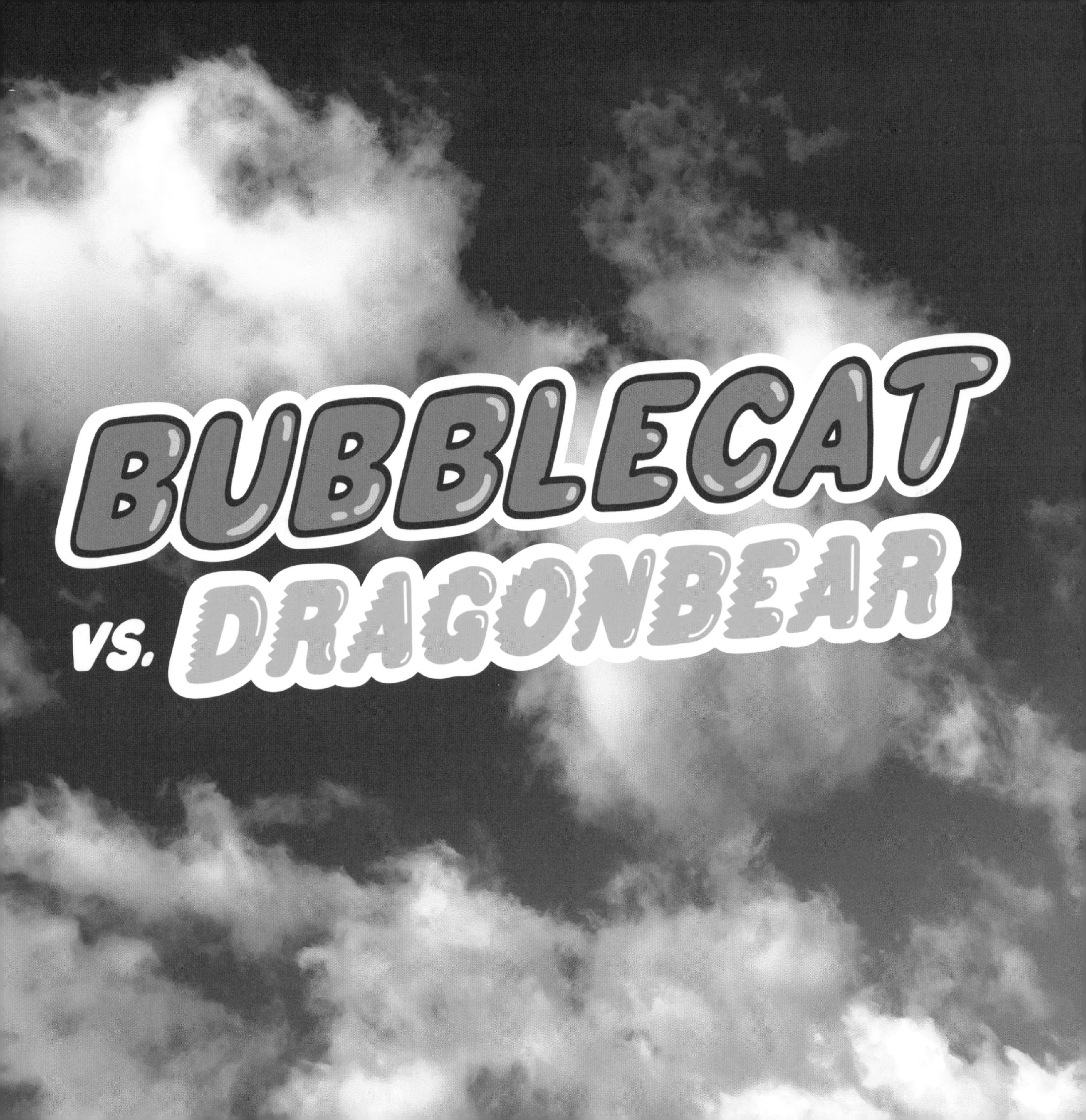

For Shaya Charmatz, Samira Charmatz,
Alan Charmatz, Dave and Iona, Priscilla Wong,
Chris Stover, and Danny Langston—SC

PENGUIN WORKSHOP
An imprint of Penguin Random House LLC, New York

First published in the United States of America by Penguin Workshop,
an imprint of Penguin Random House LLC, New York, 2022

Visit us online at penguinrandomhouse.com.

Library of Congress Cataloging-in-Publication Data is available.

Manufactured in China

ISBN 9780593223840   10 9 8 7 6 5 4 3 2 1 HH

BUBBLECAT
vs. DRAGONBEAR

by
Sean Charmatz

Penguin Workshop

I have to always be careful, because I'm a very fragile bubble. There are so many things that could poke me, so I only ever stick to the safest path. I just can't risk it.

And when Paul Porcupine comes strolling by,
then even the safe path becomes a prickly passage.

The list of things that could poke me is endless—spiked sage, barbed brambles, thorns, horns, and even a plain old pointy branch.

So I avoid anything that can hurt me.

Oh, and let's not forget to add to the list the very artistic, but extremely sharp-toothed, short-tempered, fire-breathing—

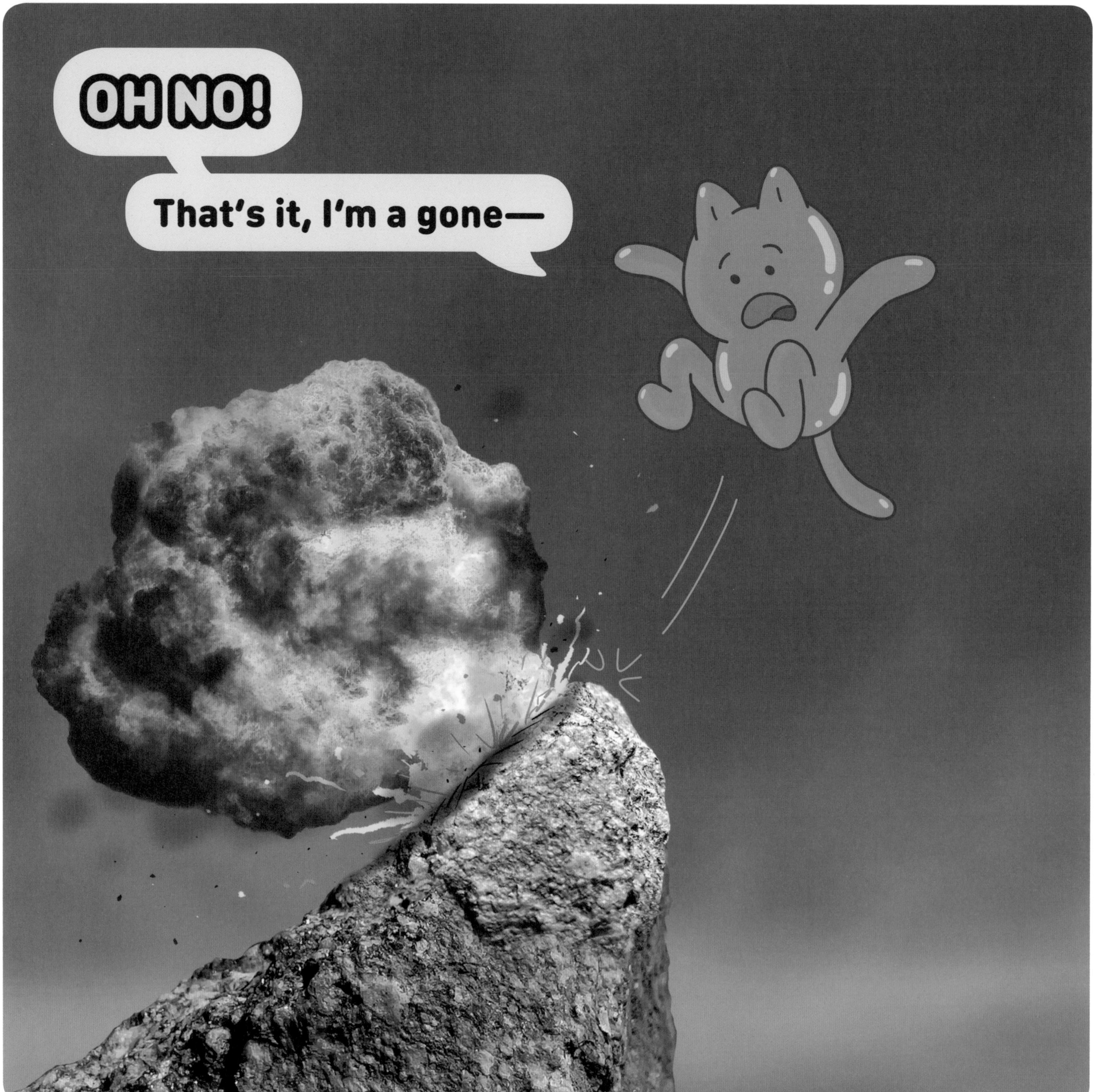
OH NO!
That's it, I'm a gone—